Barbie
IN THE
Nutcracker

FROM THE ORIGINAL VIDEO SCREENPLAY BY

LINDA ENGELSIEPEN & HILARY HINKLE

BASED ON THE CLASSIC TALE BY

E. T. A. HOFFMAN

ILLUSTRATED BY

ROBERT SAUBER

PEPPERMINT GIRL

MARZIPAN

MAJOR MINT

SNOW FAIRY

THE NUTCRACKER

FLOWER FAIRY

GINGERBREAD BOY

MOUSE KING

COLONEL CANDY

STARRING BARBIE AS CLARA

One Christmas Eve, a long time ago, a girl named Clara received a special present from her favorite aunt: a fine wooden Nutcracker. "Thank you, Auntie!" Clara cried. "He's wonderful!" But just a short time later, Clara's jealous little brother Tommy yanked the Nutcracker's arm, causing it to snap!

That night, Clara tiptoed downstairs and carefully bandaged the Nutcracker's arm. She soon drifted to sleep on the soft parlor sofa. As she dreamed, the clock began to strike midnight. *Bong! Bong! Bong!* Sparkling mist poured from a tiny knothole in the clock. *Bong! Bong! Bong!* An army of mice swarmed into the room.

*B*ong! *Bong! Bong!* The Nutcracker's eyes snapped open. He jumped up and raised his sword. *Bong! Bong! Bong!* Midnight! Clara's eyes fluttered open. She gasped at what she saw. There, beneath her Christmas tree, raged a battle between the Nutcracker and the mice!

Clara tried to help. But the Mouse King cast a spell, and Clara began to shrink until she was as small as the Nutcracker. "Only the Sugarplum Princess can undo this spell," the Nutcracker told her. "I've been searching for the princess ever since the Mouse King turned me into a Nutcracker."

Just then, an owl gave Clara a shiny locket. "When you find the Sugarplum Princess," he explained, "open the locket, and you will return home your normal size."

ogether, Clara and the Nutcracker went in search of the
Sugarplum Princess—through the knothole in the clock, then
down a sparkling tunnel that led to a magical land. Snowflakes
glittered, but it wasn't even cold! Suddenly, they were surrounded
by tiny, dancing creatures. "Snow fairies," the Nutcracker said.

Traveling on, Clara and the Nutcracker discovered a magical horse named Marzipan in a ruined gingerbread village. Riding in Marzipan's sleigh amid the broken cottages, Clara spotted a tiny doll on the ground. "Is this doll yours?" Clara asked a girl dressed in peppermint stripes. The Peppermint Girl nodded. "Who did this?" the Nutcracker asked her brother, the Gingerbread Boy. "The Mouse King's army," they answered.

And here they come!" yelled the children. Marzipan raced away for safety, leaving Clara and her friends to run from the evil mice. Suddenly, a ladder unfurled from a tree above. Racing up the ladder, they met their rescuers, Major Mint and Colonel Candy. "Let us help you find the Sugarplum Princess," said Major Mint.

eanwhile, inside the Palace of Sweets, the Mouse King sat surrounded by subjects he'd turned into stone. Frowning, he listened as Pimm the Bat told him the news: Clara and the Nutcracker were looking for the Sugarplum Princess. The Mouse King's eyes glittered. "I have a plan to stop them!" he sneered.

$\mathcal{B}$ack in the forest, Clara and the Nutcracker searched for food and water for their journey. When the Nutcracker uncovered an old well, dozens of flower fairies escaped. The fairies, who'd been trapped by the evil mice, danced to thank the Nutcracker for setting them free. Filled with delight, Clara joined the fairies' fun.

Suddenly, the ground began shaking. The Mouse King had sent a Rok Giant to attack!

The air filled with snow. No, not snow—the snow fairies! They blew on the nearby lake, turning it to ice. And Marzipan galloped back, too. "Hurry to the sleigh!" Clara cried. As the Nutcracker cracked the ice with his sword, the Rok Giant crashed into the dark, icy water.

The group traveled on into a thick, dark fog. Soon, through the mist, they spotted an island of silver and gold—and a palace that glistened like pearls! "The Sugarplum Palace!" Major Mint cried, and he led them into the castle. But suddenly the castle melted away. Clara saw that it was a trick! Her friends were trapped in a huge cage! She watched in horror as gray bats unfolded their wings and carried her friends away.

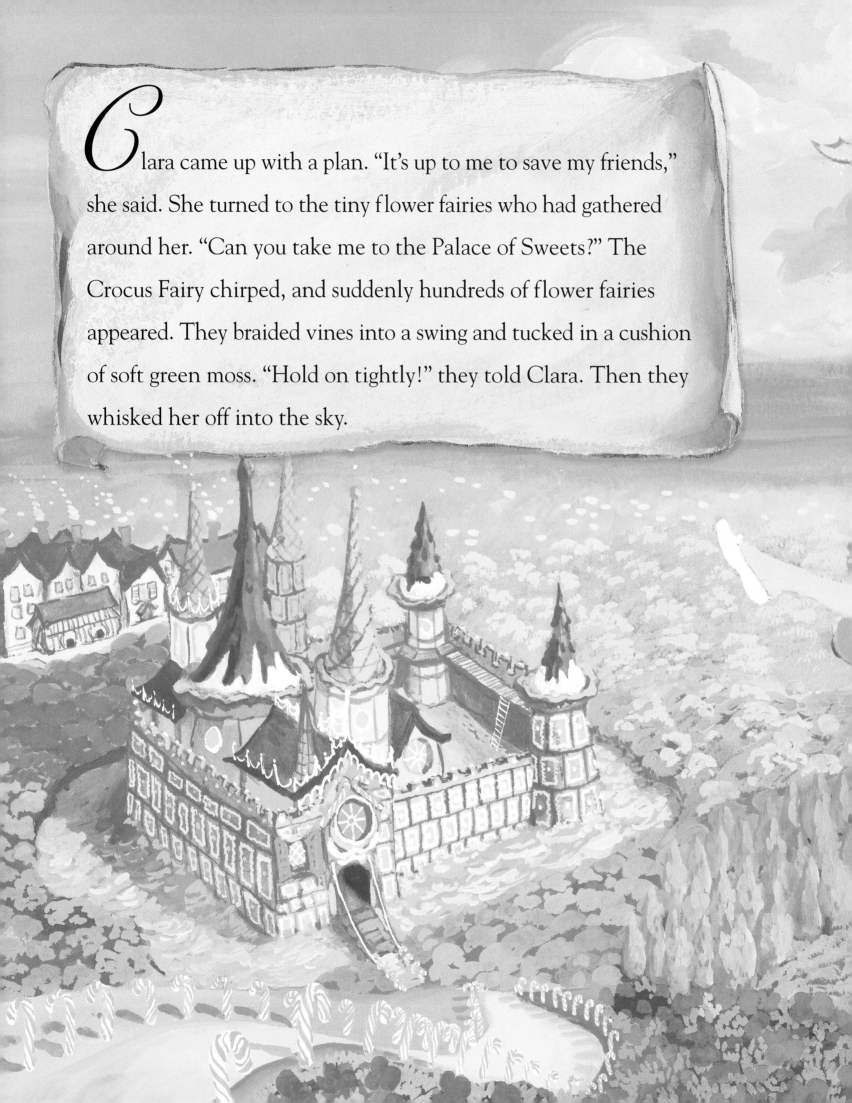

Clara came up with a plan. "It's up to me to save my friends," she said. She turned to the tiny flower fairies who had gathered around her. "Can you take me to the Palace of Sweets?" The Crocus Fairy chirped, and suddenly hundreds of flower fairies appeared. They braided vines into a swing and tucked in a cushion of soft green moss. "Hold on tightly!" they told Clara. Then they whisked her off into the sky.

When Clara reached the castle, she sneaked inside and saved her friends. The Mouse King was angered by their escape. He called to his soldiers and aimed his magic scepter. But the Nutcracker raised his sword and the blade reflected the evil magic back at the Mouse King—and he began to shrink and shrink and shrink. . . .

$\mathcal{A}$s Clara gently kissed the Nutcracker, a golden mist swirled around them. And the Nutcracker turned into . . . Prince Eric! Clara's simple nightgown transformed into a satin gown, and a golden crown appeared on her head. All around them, the stone statues turned back into people and fairies.

"You are the Sugarplum Princess," Prince Eric told an astonished Clara. "And you have broken the Mouse King's evil enchantments."

The fairies transformed the palace with magic. Everyone celebrated, then bowed as the prince was crowned king.

"Will you stay and be my queen?" King Eric asked Clara.

Clara grasped the locket around her neck. "This was supposed to take me home. But in my heart, I feel I'm already there." The teeny tiny Mouse King was not finished with his mischief, however. Pimm the Bat swooped down and stole Clara's locket and handed it to the Mouse King. And as he opened it, Clara began to fade away. . . .

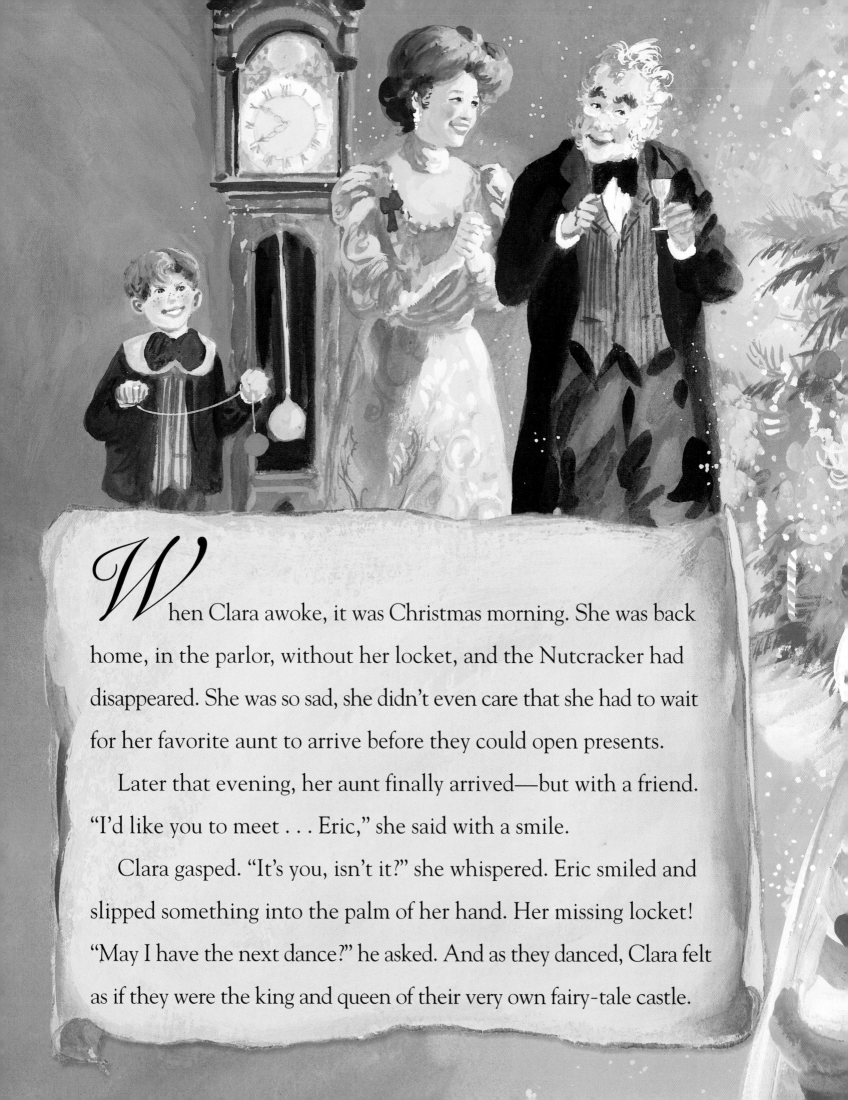

When Clara awoke, it was Christmas morning. She was back home, in the parlor, without her locket, and the Nutcracker had disappeared. She was so sad, she didn't even care that she had to wait for her favorite aunt to arrive before they could open presents.

Later that evening, her aunt finally arrived—but with a friend. "I'd like you to meet . . . Eric," she said with a smile.

Clara gasped. "It's you, isn't it?" she whispered. Eric smiled and slipped something into the palm of her hand. Her missing locket! "May I have the next dance?" he asked. And as they danced, Clara felt as if they were the king and queen of their very own fairy-tale castle.

THE END

Published by Pleasant Company Publications

© 2001 Mattel, Inc.

BARBIE and associated trademarks are owned by and used under license from Mattel, Inc.

All rights reserved. No part of this book may be used or reproduced in any manner whatsoever without written permission except in the case of brief quotations embodied in critical articles and reviews. For information, address: Book Editor, Pleasant Company Publications, 8400 Fairway Place, P.O. Box 620998, Middleton, Wisconsin 53562.

Printed in Hong Kong. Bound in China.

01 02 03 04 05 06 C&C 10 9 8 7 6 5 4 3 2 1

Library of Congress Cataloging-in-Publication data available upon request.